THE WRITER

TOM NORTH

There I was, sat on a train on my own. The train was flooded with early evening sunlight, a light yellow glow trying to convince me that the world was kinder than it was. I looked at the tops of the buildings as the train sped past.

I had been in New York for just under a year. I had gone there to study and to write. Wanting to finally follow in the footsteps of my idol. Federico García Lorca - he was a Spanish playwright and poet from the early 20th Century. He wrote a book of poems all about his time staying in America and his experience of being a young foreign man in the city.

Unfortunately I had had the opposite experience to him since being there. I felt completely uninspired by it all. I don't know why, but for me the city felt hollow and lifeless and I felt that I couldn't connect with it, or anyone in it.

I had left my entire life behind in England to come and chase this dream. For some reason I thought that once I got here, the ideas would just flow and I would finally create my masterpiece. I was in my mid twenties studying a postgraduate in English Literature. That was my pretence for being there. But really, I wanted to write my own stuff. I wanted to write my great novel or poem.

The train was clattering along, clattering as metal banged against metal. I pulled out my notebook from my pocket and tried to write down some ideas for a poem about being stuck on a train and feeling lost. Something about the train having direction, being stuck on rails, but myself feeling lost and directionless. But it all felt trite and uninteresting. I felt like I'd read it all before; everything was a tired cliche, there was no escape.

I caught the eye of a woman sitting opposite me, she was small and blonde, with a friendly, slightly chubby face. I smiled at her and she gave a gentle smile back. I hadn't really had much of a love life since being in New York either, it's like women could smell the failure on me. They just weren't interested and, in all honesty, I'm not sure I was really interested in romance at that point either. I wanted to be on my own, to be independent; I had created the idea that I was going to be a lonely starving artist; having a girlfriend didn't fit in with that fantasy. That didn't stop me craving some physical affection though - it didn't stop me from craving sex.

I was debating whether to pluck up the courage to talk to her, she kept looking up from her phone at me and was clearly trying to get my attention. I was frozen in indecision and trying to write some notes about the indecision I felt in my notebook.

Then I noticed another pair of eyes watching me write from a few seats to her left. There was a guy peering at me unashamedly through his small circular glasses. He had his arms lightly crossed and his ankle resting on his knee. He wore a brown tweed blazer and a shirt. His eyes were blue and the slight dapple of grey in his hair betrayed his age. He seemed to be somewhere in his early forties, but he still had the strength of a young man. I could see the muscles of his arms pushing through the fabric of his blazer.

He caught me looking at him but didn't even flinch. I looked for a moment and then continued writing, now making notes on strangers watching on the train. I braved another look and he was still staring, now giving a gentle smile. I had to admit it. He was handsome.

My eyes flicked back to the blonde girl who was demurely grinning at me. Why was everyone staring at me this evening? I thought.

I became slightly overwhelmed and tried to ignore them both, furiously trying to scribble out something coherent into my notebook. But something in me was suddenly feeling very alive.

"What are you writing?" I heard a deep voice bellow across the clatter of the train.

I looked up to see the girl looking over at the guy, who was staring at me expectantly.

"Oh it's nothing. Just some notes." I replied with apprehension and tried to force myself back into the pages. I could feel my cheeks starting to flush red. I don't know why, but I felt embarrassed.

"Whatever it is, it looks to be very important." He chuckled. I looked at him again, the kindness of his eyes somehow infecting me. I glanced again at the girl opposite who was starting to look slightly irritated.

"No, not important. It's just scribblings." I said and tried for a third time to turn my attention back to my notebook. The guy seemed to get the hint and remained quiet until we got to the next stop. My eyes lifted as the girl opposite got up to get off the train. Another opportunity missed.

The guy was now busy reading a book that he had pulled from his brown leather satchel. Part of me was slightly annoyed that he was no longer showing me any attention. But I didn't know why.

I glanced up and down him, taking in the strength that seemed to easily rest in every muscle of his body. He seemed unbelievably comfortable in his own skin. Like the world was made for him to sit in.

As I scanned him up and down I noticed the book he was reading. It was a play by Lorca called Blood Wedding - one of my favourites. I smiled to myself and continued scribbling, but I couldn't help glancing at him every now and then.

"Are you enjoying it?" I found myself saying across the clatter.

"Sorry?" He said as his lifted his attention from the book.

"I was just asking if you're enjoying the book."

"Yes, very much. It's one of my favourites."

"Mine too." I said. He smiled knowingly and then we sat in silence.

After another few minutes he said, "Where are you from?"

"I grew up in London."

"It's a lovely city. How did you find yourself over here?"

"Well, im here to study." I hesitated for a moment, "but really I came here to write."

"That explains the scribbling." He gestured toward my notebook.

He massaged his hands then put the book back into his bag. Then he lifted himself from his seat and came to sit next to me.

"My name is Jon." He said as he lifted his hand to shake mine.

"Im Jamie."

"What sort of thing do you like to write?"

"Well at the moment nothing at all. But I'd like to write novels and poems. It doesn't seem to be going too well at the moment."

"Writer's block?"

"You could say that." I chuckled. There was an awward silence. "What do you do?"

"I'm a lecturer actually."

"Oh great, what do you teach?"

"Well, mostly English literature, but I also run a course on creative writing."

My stomach flipped over and then plummeted down to my knees. There was me pretending to be a writer while talking to someone who really knows what he's talking about. I was so embarrassed.

"That's great. English Lit is my major."

"I teach at Columbia."

"I'm at NYU."

That felt like a relief, but I wasn't really sure why. It was good to know that I wouldn't come across him at college.

He had this really intense gaze that seemed to look right into me. I felt so exposed but also really excited.

"How are you finding New York?" He asked.

"I love it. But I have to say it's not quite living up to the hype. Not quite finding the inspirations here that I thought I would."

"Well, London has such a rich history. After that I'm sure there's little that New York can offer. Although, it is a very different city. Perhaps it's not your type of city."

"I guess so, although I don't really know what that means. I'm struggling to work out what kind of person I am exactly. I never quite felt at home in London either."

"Well, whether you felt at home there or not. It is a part of you, perhaps that would be an interesting thing for you to explore. Why do you feel so alienated by your own home?" His voice was warm and kind. But I could feel myself bristle slightly at the personal comment. "I'm sorry, that was quite an inappropriate thing to say on a first meeting. I know nothing about you. But it does seem like there's a sadness to you. I hope you don't mind me saying."

"Well, I guess I do feel a bit lost. My time here isn't

quite what I wanted it to be."

"What did you want it to be?"

"I guess I hoped I would have some adventures, find myself and work out what it is I wanted to say. But actually, I just feel more confused than ever."

"I don't want to patronise you. You seem an intelligent man. But I would say that sometimes, the confusion is the most fruitful state to be in." He smiled gently.

Those were patronising words, but I could feel their sincerity. He seemed to actually care and there was a sense that he had experienced things that I hadn't even been near to.

"Thank you." I said and another awkward silence fell between us. I could see him looking at me again, his eyes wandering over my body. I felt suddenly aware of my skin, the way it was hugged by my clothes. He seemed like he was wanting to say something, but weighing up whether he could.

"What are your plans for the evening?" He asked.

"I don't really have any. I was just heading back home from the library."

He paused for a moment and then said, "Well, perhaps you'd like to come to mine for a drink? I'd love to talk more about your work. It's always interesting to talk to another fan of Lorca."

My stomach lit up. I was excited and terrified. I'd only just met the guy and he wanted to talk to me about my writing. I honestly felt like I had nothing to say about it.

"I don't really have much to say about my work." I said.

"Well, perhaps I might have something to say about it. Why don't you take the risk? You have nothing to lose."

"I suppose you're right. It would be nice to be able to talk to someone about it. My lecturers don't seem to be much help."

"Well," he chuckled, "I'm not your lecturer and I'm not offering you private tuition. But I'm happy to be a friend to struggling writer." He patted my leg. His grip was firm, again proving the strength that lay in his body. I was six foot and spent a fair bit of time at the gym and I still felt like he could dominate me physically.

"Okay. Honestly that would be really great." I said, it did feel like a relief to have someone who seemed to understand me. I had felt so alone since being in New York.

"Mine is the next stop." He said. I nodded and smiled back at him in response and we quietly waited for the train to come to a stop.

2

We arrived in Jon's flat about twenty minutes later. My shoes hit onto the parquet floors with a satisfying tap.

"Shall I take my shoes off?" I asked.

"It's completely up to you. I'm not particular."

I gently nudged my trainers off of my feet and let my socks stroke along the floor. I placed my bag down by the coat hooks along with my jacket and made my way into the flat.

The flat oozed sophistication. Everything seemed to have class; dark wood furniture and leather sofas were everywhere. Gorgeous works of art and paintings. Shelves full of old and collectible books. I felt so at home in that place.

"Please make yourself at home." Jon said, "what would you like to drink? I was thinking of having a whiskey."

"I've never tried whiskey." I said as I nosed my way around the bookshelves in the front room as the last of the evening light filtered in from the balcony.

"It's not the easiest taste to get used to. But you're welcome to try."

"It seems like today is all about new experiences." I chuckled.

"So it would seem." He smiled as he turned toward his drunks cabinet and poured out two glasses of whiskey before handing one over to me. He placed his down on the table then said, "Excuse me while I just freshen myself up." Then he walked off, I assumed to the bathroom.

I continued looking through his book shelves. I had never seen such a great collection outside of a library, every literary classic was there. It was so exciting to see everything so beautifully lined up and cared for. This was clearly a man who had a deep love for art and literature. On the wall beside the bookcase was a painting of two naked young men, undressing by a river. I'd never seen the painting before, but there was something strangely beautiful about it.

"That's my favourite." He said as he entered back into the room.

"It's really beautiful, who's the painter?"

"I always find It's better to enjoy a painting without knowing the story behind it. Just enjoy it for what you see in front of you."

"That's a fair point. I normally get caught up in the story of the artist and what drove them to paint what they painted. I'd never thought about what that would take away from it." I said as I noticed him gently repositioning his grip on his glass.

"So, can you tell me a bit about your writing? What inspires you, what sort of themes do you like to explore?"

"Well actually that's kind of my problem. Nothing is really inspiring me at the moment. I'm finding my life to be a bit dull and meaningless. Hard to make beautiful art out of that."

"Can I read something of yours? Do you have anything with you?"

"There's some stuff on my laptop. I've got a short story I've been working on about a guy who has moved to a new place and is struggling to start a life for himself - really subtle I know." I smirked as I grabbed the laptop out of my bag and pulled up the story. I was nervous showing someone I'd never met, but at that point I was kinda desperate.

"Well, let's take a look." He said as he put on a small pair of glasses and began looking at the laptop screen.

We sat there for about 10 minutes while Jon read through the story. I could feel the tension in my body building. I couldn't stop myself from glancing over his body. I'd never seen someone look so intelligent but so physically strong. It didn't seem to match in my head.

After a while he placed his glasses down on the table and looked in my direction.

"Can I be brutally honest with you?"

"Yes, please be as honest as you need." I said, while simultaneously hoping he would lie to keep me happy.

"It sounds to me like you need a good fuck."

"Excuse me?"

"Well, the words just ooze sexual frustration and frigidity. It feel completely sexless but at the same time desperate for some kind of human contact and primal intimacy."

I didn't really know how to respond.

"There's a lot of good stuff in there. Clearly you've got the technical skill. But it feels to me like you're holding something back. I think you could find more sensuality. More carnality."

I felt completely exposed.

"The idea of sex seems to make you nervous." He said.

"Not nervous. I just, I guess I'd never really thought about it as having an impact on my writing."

"Everything is about sex. Sex is touch, feeling the pleasure of your body, finding the pleasure in holding a pen, pushing it against paper. Everything is sex Jamie. Everything is pleasurable, if you pay attention. Even the pain."

I could feel blood flush my skin. I was suddenly aware of my entire body. Even my cock began to twitch in my pants.

"I find if I lose connection to sexual pleasure, then I lose my connection to writing. Suddenly I have nothing interesting to say. It may be the same for you." His hand was resting on the leather of the sofa as he looked into my eyes. Blood continued pumping into my cock.

"It's a modest suggestion. But I'd say you need to have a good hard fuck and perhaps you'll find things less dull and uninspiring." He smiled as he pushed the laptop closed and placed it on the table. Leaning himself back into the cushion.

I laughed to try and dispel the strange tension that was building. "Well, I haven't had much success in dating since I've been here. Haven't quite got the hang on New York women."

"Well, I didn't say dating. I said fucking. You need something primal. Sweat, grunting, the slapping of skin." I swallowed hard. My penis now fully erect.

"Sounds great. But it's easier said than done."

"Perhaps." He smirked.

There was a moment of silence as he looked me up and down. I placed my hand over my crotch, hoping he wouldn't notice my boner.

"I find it's easier to find a man when it comes to a good hard fuck. Women can be a bit fussier."

"A man?"

"Yes."

"Well, that's not really my thing."

"Have you ever tried it?"

"No, but I'm straight. I've never really had the interest."

"You've got an interest in sex though? You like to shoot your load?"

"Yeah! Of course."

"I think you'll find that sex is sex. You might be surprised what a man can make you feel." He stroked the sofa with his hand. His eyes flickering with charm and mischief.

"I guess. But if I can't get a woman in bed with me I don't think I'm suddenly going to be an expert in men." I laughed.

"Don't underestimate yourself." He said confidently.

My cock was throbbing in my pants and my skin was tingling. I didn't know why, but I was so turned on I could barely breath. I looked into his eyes and took another sip of whiskey.

"Can I tell you something?" I found myself saying.

"Anything."

"My cock is rock hard." I couldn't believe my own words. I hadn't planned to say it but suddenly I was confessing myself. Laying myself out in front of him.

"Is that so?"

"I'm sorry, I don't know why I said that. It's completely inappropriate."

"The truth usually is. Don't apologise. I appreciate your frankness." He ran a finger across his bottom lip as if wiping something away then he leaned forwards. "To be brutally honest, my cock is also rock hard. I find you extremely attractive Jamie."

"You do?" I gulped.

"I do." He said with certainty.

"Well, thanks. You're not so bad yourself." I laughed awkwardly.

"Would you mind if I sucked your cock?"

"Umm…I don't know." He stayed silently waiting for my answer. Then a force in me surrendered. "Okay." I said.

"Take your pants off and take a seat."

I paused a moment and then did as he instructed.

Slowly unfastening my belt, unbuttoning my pants. I pulled them down and kicked them off, leaving my hard cock poking through my boxer briefs. Then I grabbed the waistband of my underwear and looked in his eyes for confirmation. He nodded and I pulled my underwear down letting my cock bounce free, the foreskin already pulled back over my end, my balls hanging low. I readjusted my balls and stroked my cock gently with my fingers before sitting my bare ass down on the leather of the sofa. My cock hitting onto my stomach with a satisfying slap.

"Very nice." He said and began walking over to me with an irresistible lust in his eyes.

3

Jon knelt between my legs and ran his hands up my thigh toward my cock. He dug his fingers into my pubic hair and cupped my balls with his thumb. Then he took his other hand and gently stroked along my shaft, making me twitch in anticipation.

After running his finger up and down a few times he then took all of my meat in his fists and gripped firmly. I squirmed in pleasure and let out a gasp. It felt really fucking good to finally have someone touching me. It had been a long time. Something about his strength and confidence was turning me on even more.

He took the hand that was in my pubes and pushed it up under my shirt to rub along my abs. His fingers rippling over my stomach muscles.

Then he started to slowly pump my cock, the foreskin pulling back and forth over my end. A hint of precum beginning to leak from my tip.

I pushed my head back against the armchair as the pleasure began to build. Then his strokes began to slow and I felt his tongue graze the top of my cock before his lips engulfed my end. The warmth of his mouth was unbelievable. I'd never been so turned on.

Jon then slid my whole cock into his mouth and down his throat causing me to grip onto the arm of the sofa and let out a low intense groan. Then he started working up and down my shaft with his hand and mouth, gently twisting his fist with every stroke. The pleasure was unbelievable. The gentle scratch of his stubble making the sensations even more intense.

Then he moved his hand from my abs down to my balls and began to gently massage them. No woman had ever given me a blowjob like this before. It was unbelievably intense.

As his continued the rhythmic movements, my pleasure was building to an explosion, my groans growing louder and less controllable. His pace began to quicken as he heard my groaning.

"Jon, I'm gonna come." I groaned.

Then his pace picked up even faster, the sound of his mouth sloppily sliding up and down my dick sending me over the edge. Then he pulled at my balls and my whole body began to shake as cum erupted out of my cock into Jon's throat. My entire body exploding into pleasure as my muscles tensed and released. I had never felt so alive.

Jon kept sucking up and down my shaft, swallowing every drop of my cum. Then he began to release his grip. Licking his lips, before kissing my tip. Then he let go and moved away, to sit back down on the sofa across from me.

As the euphoria began to fade from my body I slowly came back to a normal level of consciousness. Becoming aware of what had just happened and feeling a slight tickle of regret and shame, but also elation and satisfaction.

"That was really fucking good." I admitted.

"I'm glad, you certainly seemed like you were enjoying yourself. I hope you don't mind me saying, but I really enjoyed the taste of your cock."

"I'm glad." I laughed.

"So what was it like getting your first blowjob from a guy?"

"Well, I've got to confess, you certainly seemed to

know what you were doing."

"Easier to pleasure someone's dick when you have one too."

"I guess so. It really did feel incredible. I've never experienced something like that before. Never had a random hook up from the subway."

"Well, I hope you agree that it's more than a hook up. Feels like there's a real friendship and exploration to be found here."

I paused for a moment. Not sure what he was meaning.

"I don't mean a relationship. Don't panic. But like I said - it seems to me you're a bit blocked and maybe some sexual exploration with someone who knows what they're doing might be good for you?" Jon said.

"What exactly did you have in mind?"

"Well I think this was a good start, but that's only the tip of the iceberg. There are all sorts of other pleasures we could explore together. The human body is quite incredible thing to experience. Touch is an endless sensation, touching someone else is an endless mystery. I'd like to touch you more. I'd like you to touch me."

As I sat there with my semi flaccid cock begin to droop down onto the leather below me. I felt a door inside me opening up, sunshine flowing into my gut. Was I excited? I didn't know, but I felt alive. Confused for sure. Something about this situation was terrifying. But my body couldn't resist it. I wanted him - whatever that meant.

"You don't have to give me an answer now. And there's no need to rush off anywhere If you don't want to. Spend the evening with me. I'll grab you a towel, go take a shower and have a think about what you want. I've got some stuff in the fridge to make a salad. If you're interested?"

"Sure." I said. I rose to my feet, enjoying the sensation of my dick and balls swinging around freely in front of a guy with my cum in his stomach. Jon brought me a towel and I went into his bathroom. I stood for a while, staring at myself in the mirror. I couldn't understand who it was staring back. It looked like a different person. I never thought I was the type of guy to fuck other guys. To fuck random people.

Maybe I didn't know who I was at all.

My eyes kept resting on a small mole just under my cheek bone. Had it always been there? What other parts of me were always there but for whatever reason I had never seen. It seemed utterly unbelievable to me that I could spend twenty five years living, and still not know a thing. And still notice something new in myself. I felt endless.

The heat from the shower helped to ground me back into my body. The feel of the water rushing down my skin burned me into existence. I felt comforted. Maybe the world wasn't as harsh and horrible as it seemed. New York seemed hard and tough and I felt soft and vulnerable. Maybe something about that was sexy. Maybe the interplay of soft and hard was where the pleasure was really at.

My cock began to swell again at the thought of Jon touching me. At the thought of touching him. As I watched the water stream down my abs and onto my slowly hardening dick it became very clear to me that I had to stay. Jon had something to show me and I really wanted to learn.

4

I came out of the bathroom with my towel wrapped around my waist to find Jon serving up some dinner on the large glass table. He'd laid out two wine glasses and a bottle of white. He was in the kitchen finishing up the salad. I made my way back into the living room and put my clothes back on. It felt strange to be fully dressed again and I kind of missed the freedom of letting it all hang free with this guy.

Then I made my way into the kitchen.

"Can I help out with anything?"

"Absolutely not. Take a seat and relax. How was the shower?"

"Really great. This is all a bit surreal but it certainly helped to level my head a bit."

"Nothing like a bit of hot water to level the senses."

"Are you sure you don't mind me staying around for a bit? I don't know why but I just feel really relaxed here."

"I wouldn't have offered if I didn't mean it. It's nice to have some company, especially the company of an intelligent and handsome man."

I couldn't stop myself from chuckling, "You really are quite the charmer."

"I do my best." His confident smile wrapped across his face as he took the last of the food onto the table. There was salad, olives, cheese and bread. A real Mediterranean selection. It looked gorgeous.

"Please, sit down. I'll just get some cutlery."

I sat down at a corner of the table where one of the plates had been set - leaving the head of the table for Jon. After a few moments he came to join me and served me up some food.

"Thank you so much. This looks amazing."

"Glass of wine?"

"Yes please." I took a small sip and felt my body relax into the silence. "So, have you always lived in New York?"

"No, I was a small town country boy from Alabama, believe it or not. I've managed to lose the accent, but sometimes I still notice it. It's very difficult to eradicate your roots."

"Why would you want to?"

"Let's just say I wasn't the biggest fan of Alabama growing up. I could never quite be myself there. It may be where I'm from but it certainly never felt like where I was going. Although, admittedly I do find myself thinking of it fondly sometimes. There is something quite romantic about the rural life. I always had a good relationship with the animals we kept. Especially our dog. Very difficult to keep animals in a high rise in New York."

"Maybe a hamster?"

"That's always an option." He laughed, gently.

"You must feel similar. I'd imagine New York is quite the contrast to the UK. Such a small island must feel much more homely than the spiralling states."

"Yeah, there's definitely a difference. No matter where you are in the UK, you're still close to home. It feels like there's no escape. It always used to drive me mad."

"Why did you want to escape?"

"I don't really know. I guess I felt similar to you. I never felt like who I was quite fit in with the rest of my family. My sisters seemed to want a different life to me and they seemed to be interested in different things. None of my family would talk to me about art or books or writing. Everything felt much more surface level. It sounds judgemental when I say it like that but…"

"It's not a judgement. It's just a reality - some people are interested in art and some people are not. That's just a fact. But it can be difficult to be the one of who feels something that other people don't. It's very isolating. And the danger is that you learn to shut off that part of yourself just to fit in."

"Is that what you did?"

"Certainly. It took me a long time to truly connect with myself. To connect with my wants, to connect with my desires. The body has endless depths and the flesh wants to be touched. But sometimes it can be hard to listen."

He took a sip of his wine and continued to eat, pointing his fork into the flesh of a cherry tomato.

"I think I know the answer to this question. But have you have experimented with anal play?" Jon asked casually. I felt anxiety rise up in me, I didn't even really know what he meant - but I could imagine.

"No I haven't. Not sure I like the idea of having something up my arse."

"I admit it doesn't sound that appealing on first hearing. But it's surprisingly pleasurable." His eyes lingered on mine as he took another bite.

"What exactly does it entail?"

"Well, there are all sorts of ways to explore. A tongue, a finger…" he paused for a moment, "A dick."

"Is that something that you enjoy?"

"There's nothing like the feeling of another man's dick inside you. It if it hits the prostate in just the right spot the pleasure is incomparable. But I also love fucking someone myself. There's very little I don't enjoy."

"Doesn't it hurt?"

"It can do, at first. But once you relax and get into it it feels quite the opposite. No pressure to try anything you don't want to. In fact no pressure to do anything sexual with me at all. But I get the feeling that you're curious."

"Maybe a little." I confessed reluctantly.

"Pleasure and pain are more linked than you might think. I'm sure you know this on some level already. Some pretty painful experiences have led you to my flat, and you certainly seemed to be feeling a lot pleasure when your cock was in my mouth."

I didn't respond, I just smiled at him knowingly, again my attention being drawn to the strength of his arm muscles.

"Would you let me lick your asshole?" Jon asked.

My cock immediately hardened at the thought of it and I had no idea why.

"No need to answer. I'm going to have a quick shower myself and if you are interested in experiencing the pleasure of my tongue again. You can take your clothes off and wait for me in the bedroom. All fours makes it easier." Jon said and then confidently rose to his feet and walked off into the bathroom, undoing his pants as he went.

I was left alone again, with a huge erection bulging through my pants. Yet again. This guy was having the strangest effect on me. The way he spoke so matter of factory around sex was such a turn on. I didn't even know if it was him that was turning me on or just his honesty and his attitude. It felt at that moment that I would do absolutely anything he wanted.

I nervously rose to my feet and searched around the flat for his bedroom. I found it. He had a huge bed, wooden floors, floor length mirrors covering a wall full of wardrobes. There was a small brass figure of some sort of naked Greek figure wrestling a snake. Hercules maybe? I couldn't be sure.

Being in his room and knowing what he wanted turned me on even more. I hesitated one last time, before completely removing all of my clothes. I looked at myself in the mirror. My cock was rock hard and my body was looking pretty good. All that time in the gym looked like it was paying off. There was a horny smile plastered across my face. I was excited!

I looked at the bed, then climbed on top leaning my elbows and knees into the soft covers leaving my arsehole up in the air and completely on display.

5

Moments later I heard the shower stop and heard Jon's footsteps as he entered the room. I glanced back over my arse cheeks at him as he came in. He was standing in the doorway wet and completely naked. His huge cock dangling between his legs. He was even bigger than I was. My dick twitched as it hung between my legs. I felt like I was in some sexual alternate dimension where I could do absolutely anything that I desired. And what I desired - was him.

"Good boy." He said as he stood staring at my hole.

"I aim to please."

He walked over to me. The sight of his dick and balls swinging as he walked was one of the best things I had ever seen in my life. When he arrived at my arse, he gently grabbed a cheek with one hand and then gripped it hard. Then his lifted his hand and grazed it from the bottom of my back down across my hole, then to my balls which he tickled with the tips of his fingers.

"You ready for this?" He asked.

"I'm ready."

Then his mouth lowered to my arsehole as his lips engulfed my puckered little hole, sucking at it before releasing his tongue to probe around the outside.

My whole body shivered with the sensation of his tongue. He circled around the hole a few times before pushing himself inside of me, causing me to gasp and arch my back, grabbing the sheets to keep my grip on reality.

He released his mouth and then licked from my balls up to my hole again before shoving his tongue back inside me. He feasted on my boy pussy for what felt like an eternity. Then I felt his hand come up and start teasing my hole with his finger.

"Ready for more?"

"Give it to me." I was feeling brave.

His finger started to push past my pucker as his other hand reached around and began to pump my cock. I felt myself peeling open, my body inviting his fingers in, begging for the pain of it. It stung, but I didn't want it to stop.

"How's it feel?"

"It's supposed to hurt right?"

"Just breath into it. Trust me."

I did trust him, I didn't know why, but at that moment I would trust him with my life. He kept his finger still in me while I breathed in and out, allowing my body to relax. Then his kissed my asscheek and continued pumping his finger slowly in and out of me.

A spot in my arse felt like liquid gold every time he poked into me. The pleasure was unbelievable.

"It feels good. Really good." I said.

"I'm glad." My eyes fixed onto the figure of Hercules in front of me. The snake wrapping around his muscles, it's fangs bared. His muscles were rippling, he looked as though he could tear the snake in half. It struck me just how beautiful the male body was, the strength of it was irresistible.

I felt like I was the snake, wrapped around Jon's arm, I was nothing compared to his strength. He could snap me if he wanted to. He could kill me. I wanted him to kill me.

"I want more."

"Are you sure?" He asked.

"I'm sure. Fuck me."

Jon rose to his feet, "If you want to stop. Just let me know. I'm quite big for a first timer. I'll go slow."

Jon removed his finger from me, my ass stinging once again. He went to his bedside table and put a condom on himself and lathered his cock in lube. He really was huge, I might have been overestimating my abilities, but at that point it didn't matter. I wanted to be taken, to be controlled. I wanted it to hurt.

I felt his tip touch onto my hole and it felt like a circuit finally connecting. My whole body lit up, every sensation was trebling in intensity. Then I could feel him slowly pushing his rod into my hole. I felt tight, so fucking tight. It hurt more than I can say.

"Breath." Jon said as he stopped pushing. He could obviously hear my wincing. I looked at the muscles on my arms as they tensed. I focused on my breath, and on releasing all the muscles in my body. Again the statue of Hercules came to my mind. There was something about it that was comforting. Somehow I felt held and safe. I just to had to let myself go and it would all be taken care of.

Jon began pushing again. His cock slowly slid inside of me, filling my virgin arse with his thickness. It felt like I was being ripped apart. My eyes rested on the brass of the statue. I surrendered. The pain slowly began to melt into the most unbelievable pleasure as I noticed Jon's balls pushing up against my own. His whole cock was inside me and he was grasping both of my arse cheeks, pushing his hips right into me. He stayed motionless allowing me to breath and relax into the size of him.

The feeling of his skin against mine was so comforting, I felt like he was completely in control and that's all I wanted.

"Just tell me when you're ready." He spoke.

I could feel drops of sweat beginning to form on my back already. The feeling was so intense I felt I would explode. My cock twitched, my hole to tightened and Jon let out a low groan that was irresistible.

"I'm ready. Do whatever you want with me." I said.

Then it began. Jon pulled his cock almost all the

way out and then started to thrust himself in and out of me. His tip hitting my sweet spot with every single thrust. He was slow and passionate, running his hands up and down my back as his pushed in and out of me. A golden glow of pressure was building inside me.

The slapping of his thighs against my arse cheeks was sending me over the edge and I was beginning to lose a sense of where I started and he began. It felt like we were one hot mess of flesh and sweat and pleasure.

His grunted began to deepen as his pace quickened. His thrusts becoming harder and more regular. I had to grab onto the sheets even tighter to stop myself from flying forwards and his grips on my hips got even stronger as he pulled me into him.

"Fuck, this feels incredible. Your cock feel amazing."

"Shut up, fuck boy. You talk when I want you to."

I hadn't expected the words from him. But they turned me on even more. I wanted him to dominate me, I wanted to be his fuck toy. And I knew that beneath this performance was the sweet man who had made me salad only moments ago. This was all part of the game, all part of the thrill and I trusted him.

"I'm sorry, I'm you're fuck boy. I'll do whatever you want."

He leant down to my ear and bit before whispering, "I know you will. You have no choice."

He slammed into me even harder, my hips bucking up to meet his thrusting. Then he flipped me onto my back so I could get a good look at his body. He was covered in sweat, he had dapples of hair over his chest and abs which were perfectly defined. This guy clearly spent a lot of time at the gym. He hooked my legs under his arms and brought his face up to meet mine as he counted to pummel my hole into oblivion making me squeal like a pig. Nothing else in the world mattered, all I wanted was for him to fuck me forever. How had I never experienced something so fucking good before?

He slowed his thrusts enough for me to get my breath, then he asked, "Can I kiss you?"

"Yes you can." I answered.

Then as his thrusts continued in a slow passionate

rhythm he brought his lips down to mine and we kissed the most passionate open mouthed kiss I had ever experienced. Our mouths intertwined and our tongues licked all over each other as I tasted him. Our mouth stayed clamped together as his thrusts picked up pace again. His grunted reaching a fever pitch.

"I'm going to cum soon." He said.

"I want your cum." I replied. With that permission his thrusts became more frantic and his grunts became higher pitched until the feeling hit me of his cock switching inside me, pumping into my hole. I kinda wished he wasn't wearing the condom.

The sound he made was so guttural and animal that it nearly made me cum there and then. But to be honest, the pleasure had been so intense that I wasn't even sure I needed to cum. I already felt satisfied. As he thrust the last of hit cum into me his movements and breaths began to slow. Then he kissed me one last time and pulled his huge cock out of me. Leaving me feeling empty and wishing he could stay inside of me forever.

6

After he came he pulled the covers over us and he pulled me into the warmest embrace I had ever experienced and we both drifted of to sleep. I felt so safe and held and like nothing in the world could ever be a problem. Jon could protect me from anything.

I woke up in the middle of the night, watching the light form the city drifting in through the blinds of his bedroom window. Jon's arms were still wrapped around me, the feeling of his warm skin reminding me that I was not alone. I couldn't help but wonder what would happen after tonight. How would he be with me in the morning? I kinda felt embarrassed, I'd let him fuck me. I couldn't believe it. What if he wanted more? I even let him kiss me. Maybe I was leading him on?

Hell, I hadn't agreed to anything, all I did was have some fun. I told him I was straight he couldn't have expected more from me than a fuck. He was lucky to even have that from a straight guy.

I could feel his cock pushing into my back. It felt like he was hard. This guy had some sexual appetite, he even got an erection in his sleep. The thought of his cock pressing into me made my dick immediately go hard again and I found myself pushing my arse back into his cock.

This was crazy, there I was calling myself a straight guy and all I could think about was this guy's cock.

As I lay there naked, the world started to seem a bit more interesting, I felt words coming to my mind. Words that I never thought I'd think, feelings I never thought I'd feel. I think I actually felt happy laying there in his arms.

"Jon?" I said as I turned my head towards him. "Are you awake?"

"Are you okay?" He grumbled back, half asleep.

"I'm feeling a bit confused."

"What is it?"

"Well, what do you see this as?"

"What do you mean?"

"I mean, what is it you want from me? Do you see this just as a fling?"

"You don't need to panic. Sex doesn't have to mean anything more than two people enjoying each other's bodies. I don't need anything from you."

For some reason my stomach sank when he said that. I was so scared that he would expect more of me, but now that he had said that he didn't. I was disappointed. What was wrong with me?

"I've never felt so free before. I've always kept sex at a bit of a distance to be honest. I've always felt a bit ashamed of it."

"No need to feel shame. We're animals, we can fuck and suck and do whatever we want. When we want. As long as the other person agrees of course. For the record - I am happy to fuck whenever you want." I could make out his grin through the darkness.

"Are you trying to turn me on?" I asked.

"Is it working?" He replied. I leaned in and pressed my lips once again to his, letting my whole naked body push into him. Our hard cocks meeting in the middle as we began to grind against each other. I loved that his dick was so big, I loved that his dick was just as strong and muscular as the rest of him.

We kissed and rubbed ourselves together until yet again I lost track of who was who. Then he brought his hand down and began to rub my cock up and down. A gasp escaped my mouth as my body convulsed at the feeling. He grinned and bit my lip before pumping my dick even faster. I grabbed his dick in response like it was a competition, stroking him into a frenzy to see if I could make him cum even faster. I laughed and groaned as we pushed each other over the edge. With ever stroke I could feel his foreskin pulling back and forth, making it harder to keep myself from exploding all over him.

Then both of our wrists were moving in a blur

while our mouths consumed each other. Eventually it was too much and I shot out ribbons of cum all over his hand as I screamed out his name. Then I felt his hot juices falling on my arm and my hands as he groaned that low guttural growl that I recognised from earlier. He gently rubbed our cum together onto my abs and cock as he continued to kiss me.

"I've never felt like this before." I found myself saying.

"How do you feel?" He asked.

"I don't know, my whole body feels alive. My insides are glowing."

"I love you too." He said.

What the fuck? What did he say? My stomach sank again. Did he just say he loved me? I thought he said he didn't want anything more from me? What did that even mean? I didn't know how to respond so I just pretended that I hadn't heard him. His kissed me once more then cleaned us both up with a towel that was next to the bed. Then he pulled me back into a hug and went back to sleep.

My eyes were wide open, staring out into the darkness of the room. First thing in the morning, I would have to get out of there. Maybe it had all been a huge mistake.

I woke up in the morning in an empty bed. Jon was nowhere to be seen. After tossing snd turning for a while worrying about what he had said I had eventually fallen to sleep and I felt strangely rested. Apart from the knot in my stomach from thinking about his words. I still couldn't believe he had said that.

I turned over and looked around the room for signs of Jon, but he was nowhere to be seen. I felt my morning wood throbbing beneath the covers and I was tempted to sort myself out. But the sexual freedom I was feeling yesterday had been stopped in it's tracks. I now felt like I'd made a huge mistake.

I climbed out of the bed and put all of my clothes back on feeling the inhibitions that I had lost slowly returning. It had felt so good while it had lasted, but I suppose that reality always returns to bite you in the ass. And here I was in some random guys apartment, after letting him fuck my brains out all night. I really had no idea how any of it had even happened.

Once my clothes were on I went out tf the bedroom to search for Jon, but he was nowhere to be seen. On the dining table I saw my laptop sitting pride of place, with a note of top of it. My head cocked in confusion as I walked over to it. I lifted the note in my hands and read, 'I had to leave early for work. I wanted to let you sleep. I think you should take the day to write. I'll be out all day. Help yourself to anything you need. Jon x"

I felt anger erupt in my stomach. He expected me to stay there all day and write? He expected me to feel normal after all that had happened? What was this game that he was playing? I wasn't his toy, I wasn't his pet project. I found myself screwing up the note an throwing it to the floor.

I looked out of the window, the city looked so beautiful from up there. I could see the corner of Central Park in the distance. I could see cars flowing through the streets. From up there everything seemed more serene and more delicate, the hard rough exterior of the city seemed to have lost its edge. Like I could see it all with more clarity and I wasn't as scared of it. The words that were filling my mind the night before started flooding my brain again.

I sighed and looked back to my laptop. I had trusted Jon. Maybe I just had to continue trusting him? What did I have to lose?

I reluctantly walked over to the laptop, opened it up and began to type.

Time melted and by the end of the day I had

written thousands of words. They just seemed to flow out of me like I had never experienced before in my life. I couldn't believe it. I had actually written! And I had written things that I actually liked, it felt like I finally had something to say,

I looked up from the laptop and realised that it was dark outside again. I had spent the whole day at Jon's place, eating his food, drinking his coffee and writing. Writing about him. I was embarrassed to admit it. But he had inspired me. He had awakened something in me that I didn't even know existed. I felt ashamed and excited all at the same time.

The door to the apartment opened with the sound of keys jingling. My stomach dropped to my feet as I panicked and shut my laptop closed. My face flushed red and I immediately wanted to bolt for the door.

As Jon walked around the corner he placed his satchel on the floor and looked at me with a tentative smile.

"I'm glad you're still here." He said.

"I don't quite know what happened. I hadn't intended to stay."

"Is that so? Well I'm glad that you did nonetheless. Was it a productive day?" He nodded towards my laptop.

"It actually was, I don't know what came over me."

He gave me a knowing smile then walked into the kitchen to start unpacking some grocery shopping that he had brought.

"Would you like some food?" He asked.

"I should really get going."

"There's no pressure to leave. Stay for as long as you like. It's quite nice having some company around the place."

I remained silent. Jon must have sensed that something was up because he came to the door and gave me a searching look.

"Are you okay?" He asked.

"I'm just freaking out a little bit. This is all brand new, I've never done anything like this before and then suddenly I meet a random guy on the subway then his dick inside me and now I feel like I'm living at your house and suddenly I'm able to write and last night you…"

"Last night I what?"

I stayed silent again.

"Are you freaking out about what I said?" He asked

"Maybe."

"Listen, I was just responding to what felt right in the moment. I could feel the intensity of your emotions and it felt like that's what you were saying to me. In that moment, it felt true to me as well. I mean, who knows? We have only just met each other. And I really did mean it when I said that I don't expect or need anything from you. If you want to leave right now and never talk to me again, then that is fine. I want whatever is best for you. For whatever reason, for better or for worse, I think you are a very special person and I care for you very much. If you want to stay here and explore that, then that would be great. If you want to leave, then I understand."

I could feel the muscles in my body start to relax. "It's just that it's brand new, and things are happening before my mind even has a chance to process it. My feelings are stronger than I even know what to do with. But it feels like something in me is waking up."

He smiled then walked over to me and pulled me into a hug. The strength of his arms crushing me into comfort and safety.

"I understand." He said.

I lifted my head off of his chest to look into his face, then I couldn't stop myself from kissing him. My hands searching up and down his back.

Jon broke the kiss, held my cheeks and looked at me, "Want to explore some more?" He said.

"What did you have in mind?"

"I think it might be time for you to fuck me." He

grinned.

My cock immediately went hard. He wanted me to shove my dick inside him? Suddenly any worry I had disappeared into erotic anticipation.

He walked over to the back of the couch and dropped his pants, leaving only his shirt and tight white underwear on display. I took his invitation and walked over to him running my hands along his arse.

I pushed my finger through the fabric of his underwear to his hole. I was so horny I wanted to tear them off straight away.

"C'mon big boy. What are you waiting for? I want you to fuck me."

I didn't need to be asked twice - although I had been.

I grabbed as his underwear and found myself ripping through the fabric, exposing his bare arse. It was soft and tanned. I grabbed at his cheeks between his underwear that was now hanging in tattering off of him. Then I pulled down my pants and underwear letting my hard cock bounce free and began to tease it against his puckered hole.

He had his arms resting on the top of the couch as he wiggled his butt onto the tip of my cock. He was really hungry for it.

"Stay there, I'm getting the lube."

"Don't bother with the condom." He said, "Unless you want it. I've been recently tested."

I wanted to fuck him raw more than anything, I hadn't slept with anyone since being in New York, so I was clean too. I grabbed the lube from the bedroom and quickly smeared it up and down my cock, groaning at the pleasure of the stroking. Then I poured a dollop onto his hole and massaged it in with my finger.

Finally, I lined my cock up to his hole and began to push, feeling his pucker slowly peeling away, letting me into that warm wetness. I groaned at the feeling of his hole enveloping my cock, he was consuming me and it felt fucking incredible. I squeezed his cheeks and shivered at the sound of his moaning.

"That's it. I want you deep inside me." He grabbed my hip with one hand and pulled me all the way into him.

"Now fuck me." He said. I couldn't believe how good it felt, there was no way I was going to last very long. He was so tight.

"I'm not gonna last."

"It doesn't matter. Just fuck me."

I grabbed onto his hips and began shoving my cock in and out of his hole. Grunting with every push and feeling my cock throbbing into a frenzy. Going raw felt amazing, I could feel every inch of his hole on my shaft. I could feel his sweet spot hitting against my tip with every thrust.

"Fuck, you feel so good." I grunted.

"I love your dick. Fill me with your cum."

I continued pumping away, out skin slapping together until finally I could feel the orgasm build. My balls tightened as my thrusts quickened in pace and before I knew it I was shooting everything I had into his hole, grabbing onto his shoulder and hip to keep me from falling over as the pleasure washed through my entire body.

My thrusting slowed and my cock continued to twitch inside of him, letting out every last drop of cum that I had. Then I slowly pulled myself out of him and stood to look at my handy work. He looked so fucking hot, bent over, ripped underwear and my cum slowly oozing out of his hole. I could do this forever, I thought to myself.

Later that evening we were both sat at the diner table enjoying some pasta that Jon had made for both of us.

"Listen, this has been the craziest twenty four hours of my life. But for whatever reason, I do have feelings for you. And I don't really want this to end." I confessed.

"It doesn't have to end." Jon smiled at me. "You stay here for as long as you need and we'll see where things go. And if you want to escape back to yours for a while and then come back here, that's fine. Whatever this is, it's ours, we can do with it whatever we please. As long as we keep fucking." He grinned a devilish grin.

"Oh don't worry about that. I've got a feeling we'll be fucking for a long time to come." I smiled as I took a bite of pasta.

I looked into Jon's eyes and allowed the happiness to wash through me. Life really wasn't so bad after all. It was tough to be vulnerable with someone, to let them help. But it in the end, without that, there wasn't much else to live for.

I hope you enjoyed the book!
I'm an independent author so your
feedback is really valuable. Please leave a
review if you can or feel free to drop me
some personal feedback to:
tomnorthauthor@gmail.com
If you would like to sign-up to my
mailing list for offers and news on future
releases please follow the link:
https://mailchi.mp/1613c8979d1a/tom-
north-narratotr
Thanks for reading!
Xx

PS. Please continue reading for a sample
of some of my other work.

It's was David's first day in his dorms at college. The day he'd been waiting for. He had been desperate to escape his hometown and finally get some independence. To finally work out who he was and what he wanted from his life.

To finally move out into the world where people didn't know him as the son of a cop, where he didn't have to watch his every move in case his Dad would disapprove. And he did it. He was finally free of his parents and their watchful eyes.

David was in his new room, carefully packing away all of his belonging, finding just the right place for everything. He put his underwear neatly into his top draw, tucking a packet of condoms in the corner - dreaming that he'd find a moment to use them before too long. He was still a virgin. But hopefully not for too much longer.

He moved on to his bookshelf, pulling out several novels from different genres. A collection of fiction he'd read over and over again, until he'd memorised it like an old friend. He set these aside, along with some other older books he'd collected over the years.

He finished up and then made his way to the mirror. Observing himself in his new space. His brown hair looked reasonably tidy, a slight fringe tickling his forehead. Brown eyes looking full of hope.

His phone chimed softly from his bag, pulling him from his thoughts. He grabbed his phone, opening his messages quickly. A single message from 'Hey, you ignoring me?', followed by several missed calls from his best friend, Shawn.

Chuckling to himself while sending back a quick reply, he placed his phone back in his pocket, turning to face the rest of his belongings. His eyes lingered upon the bookshelf. There was a lot of knowledge stored in there. Knowledge about life, freedom, love. Books about self discovery, about life outside of your parent's expectations. The book were his only escape from the monotony of life back home. But now he was free, he could explore all the things he'd only ever read about. One big thing those books couldn't show him - and the only thing he really cared about right now - was what it would actually feel like to fall in love with someone, to have sex with someone. To feel someone else's body inside your own. He turned himself on just thinking about it, feeling the erection grow in his pants.

The door swung open and David's new roommate walked into the room. He was tall, probably 6 feet if David had to guess. His skin was a shade darker than David's. Black curly hair sticking out in every direction. Blue eyes scanning the room before landing on the boy in front of him. The boy he had just met. The boy he was going to spend every night sleeping beside, sharing dreams and secrets.

"Hey man," He said, moving forward toward David. The man casually threw his arms around David pulling him into a hug, "It's nice to you" He had the biggest most genuine smile David had ever seen, and he seemed to be so relaxed. His muscles moving with an ease and masculinity that made David feel even hornier. He suddenly became very aware of his erection.

"Yeah I'm David...I uh…" He managed to say, still

trying to pull away from the man's strong grip.

The guy smiled and gave David one last squeeze before stepping back.

"Nice to meet you," He replied, making his way over to his bed. Sitting down and resting his head on the soft mattress. "My name is Liam." He stretched his legs out in front of him, reaching into his hoodie pocket, pulling out a pack of cigarettes. He pulled one out, lighting it, taking a drag and blowing out the smoke gracefully. "So how are you liking the school so far?"

David nodded, sitting down on his own bed, covering his crotch with his hands "It's okay," He paused, unsure of whether to go on, "I mean I didn't expect anything less but I am kinda nervous.."

Liam chuckled lightly, "You'll do fine, don't worry about it. What classes you're interested in?" He asked, taking another drag on his cigarette.

David shrugged, "Um…History, I think I'd like to major in that. I'm good at languages though." He replied.

"Well I'm sure you can make it through," Liam

grinned, "So listen, I know we've only just met, but, sharing a room together for the whole year we should probably come up with some ground rules."

"Ground rules?"

"Yeah, just so we can agree on what we can and can't do in the space. Like girls for instance."

"Girls?"

"Yeah, girls dummy, what do we do if either of us wants to bring a girl back? I don't wanna have to kick you out. But if you're gonna be weird about me having sex in front of you."

"Sex?!" David almost shouted, dropping his hands from his crotch, his ears starting to turn pink. "What are you talking about?"

"Are you deaf? You know like…sex. With a girl," Liam replied, "Do you mind if I bring girls back? I don't want to waste my first year on campus."

David shook his head and sighed, "No no, I don't mind. You can bring whoever you want back."

Liam smiled brightly, lighting another cigarette, "Alright then, I'll let you settle in here then. I have to go talk to a few other guys so they can give me a tour."

As Liam stood up and started walking past David he reached out and took Liam's hand. Their fingers interlocked and Liam leaned in close and whispered, "Is that a boner in your pants?"

Then, he pulled back, laughed and headed towards the door. "See ya later David," He waved over his shoulder.

David was left alone in the room blood rushing to his cheeks in embarrassment, a little bit taken aback by the conversation, he was turned on a disappointed all at the same time. This Liam guy was really hot and he was going to be having sex in the room next to him. This is not exactly the fantasy he had in mind. His cock was still pulsing in his pants and currently he only had one solution.

www.ingramcontent.com/pod-product-compliance
Lightning Source LLC
Chambersburg PA
CBHW051459140726
47987CB00006B/2796